The Wish

By JULIE STARKEY

Illustrated by

Sandra Starkey Simon & Fanny Restek

'May all beings be happy and free'

Published by Windmill Grass Publishing, 2019
Text © Julie Starkey
Illustrations © Sandra Starkey Simon and Fanny Retsek

Cover and text design by Karen V. Scott
Editing by Juliet Middleton

National Library of Australia Cataloguing- in-Publication Entry
Title: The Wish / Julie Starkey;
Illustrations by Sandra Starkey Simon and Fanny Retsek

ISBN 978-0-648503-0-3 (paperback)

Target Audience: Children 4 - 8 years old
Subject: Animal Rights–Juvenile Fiction

Morella was my pet corella.
We danced and sang and talked together.
I was young, I wasn't wise,
Her life looked good through my innocent eyes.
When Morella died she was very old
And another life story began to unfold.

It rained that day I opened the door.
I lifted her gently from the cage floor.

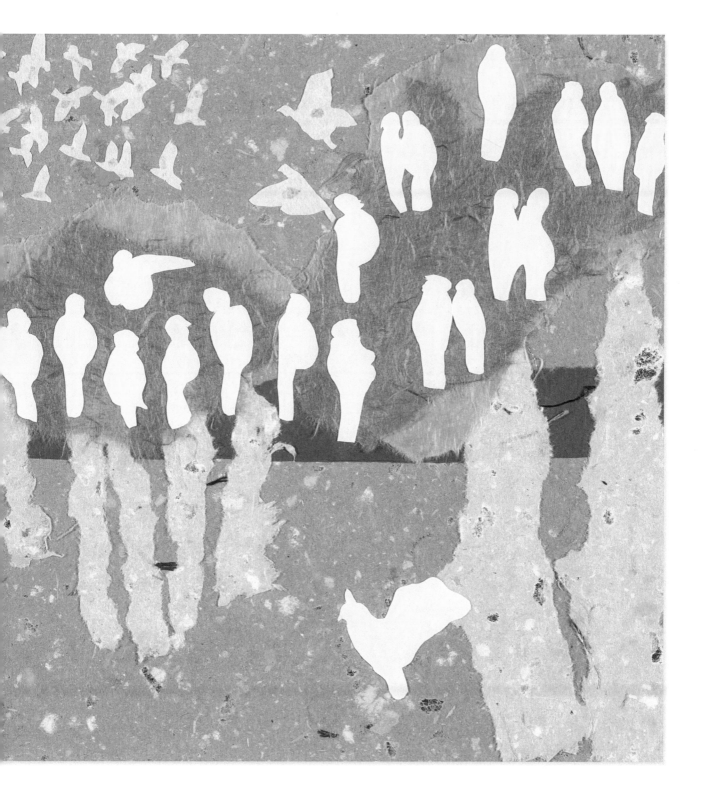

'We buried her outside beneath the trees'
While above in the heavens blew a welcoming breeze.
She never had babies, never flew high,
Had always been missing from the flock in the sky.

That night when I lay in my comfortable bed
Aware of the spirits about my head,
I thought of Morella and wished her goodbye:
'High and happy and free may you fly.'

I started to think of other animals too,
Stuck in a cage or trapped in a zoo.
It was then I realised that I could make
Life changing wishes to erase their heartache.

I put aside being selfish, thoughtless and greedy
And made a wish for five animals who were needy.

'Five animals out there, who want to be free
Your wish will be granted, just wait and see.'

Over the land in a barn was a battery chook
Closed doors and no windows – take a look.

Bred not to go broody; no room to scratch.
"I wish ... I wish ... I could lift the latch."

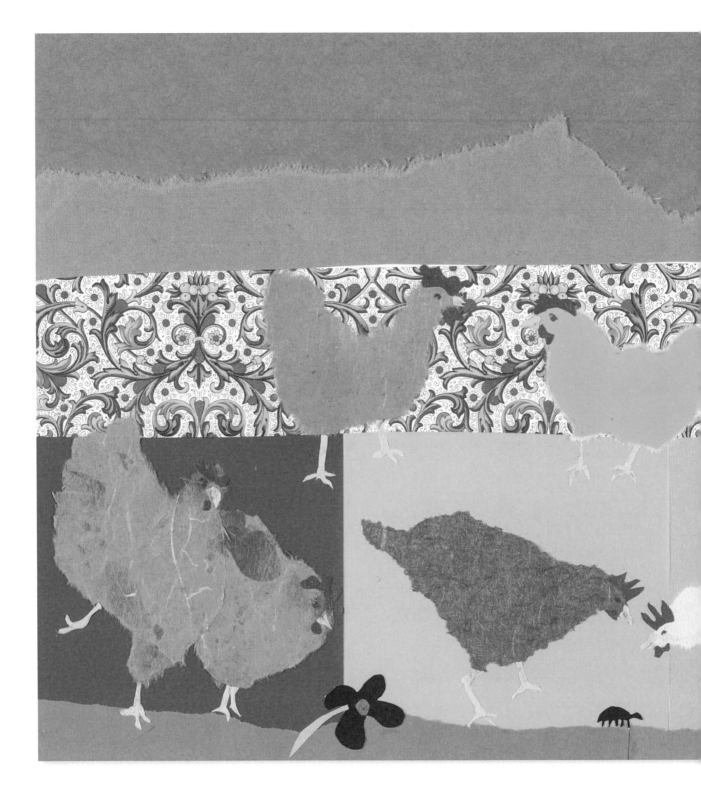

Chooky opened her eyes
And ... surprise, surprise:

She was a free-range hen
In a run of just ten.

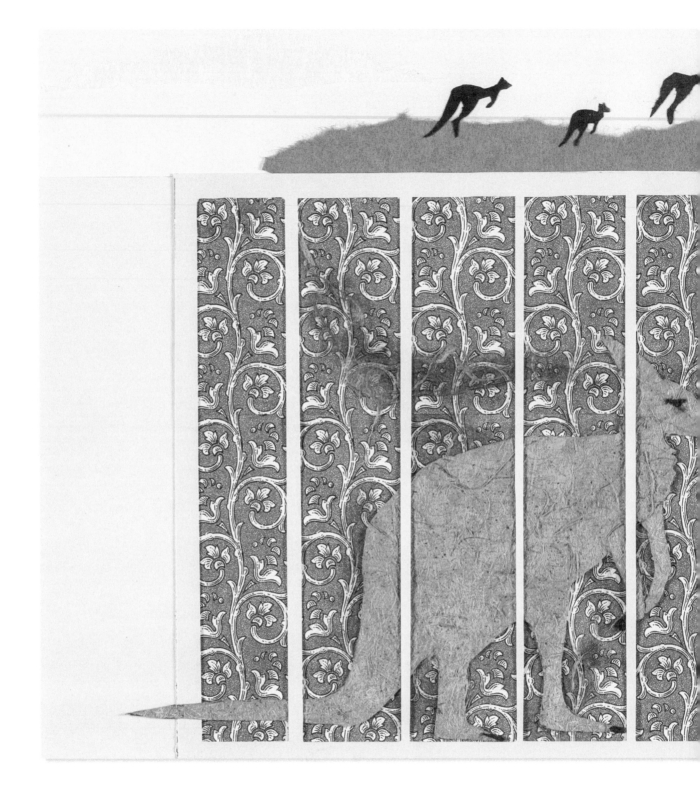

Over the land in a zoo was a kangaroo,
Surrounded by bars, he couldn't get through.

'I need desert air; I need more space.
I wish ... I wish ... with my friends I could race.'

Kanga opened his eyes
And ... surprise, surprise:

He was in Central Australia
Surrounded by flies.

Over the land in a circus was a beautiful horse,
Trotting in circles, the same boring course.

His steps were too small, his neck was all bent,
'I wish ... I wish ... I was out of this tent.'

Horsey opened his eyes
And ... surprise, surprise:

He was galloping free,
His steps the right size.

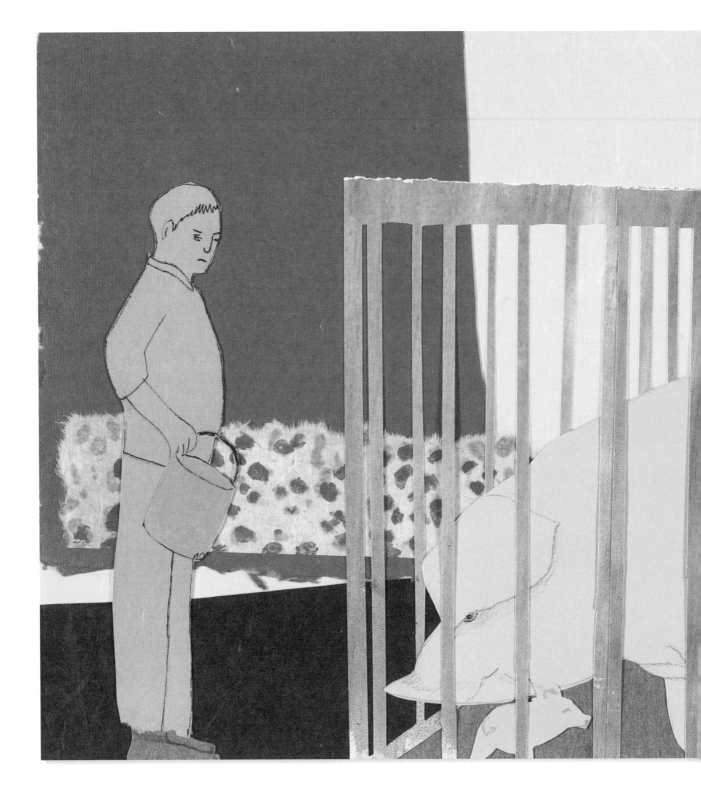

Over the land in a farm lay a large mother pig,
Crammed into her stall, no room to jig.

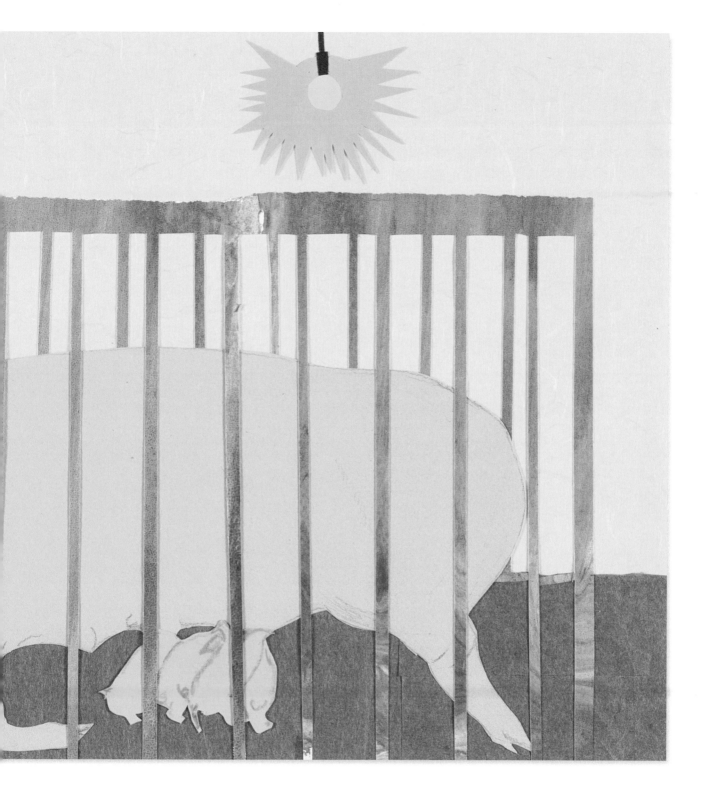

She bit at the bars, she yearned to be free.
'I wish ... I wish ... for my piglets and me.'

Piggy opened her eyes
And ... surprise, surprise:

She was down by the creek,
Piglets making mudpies.

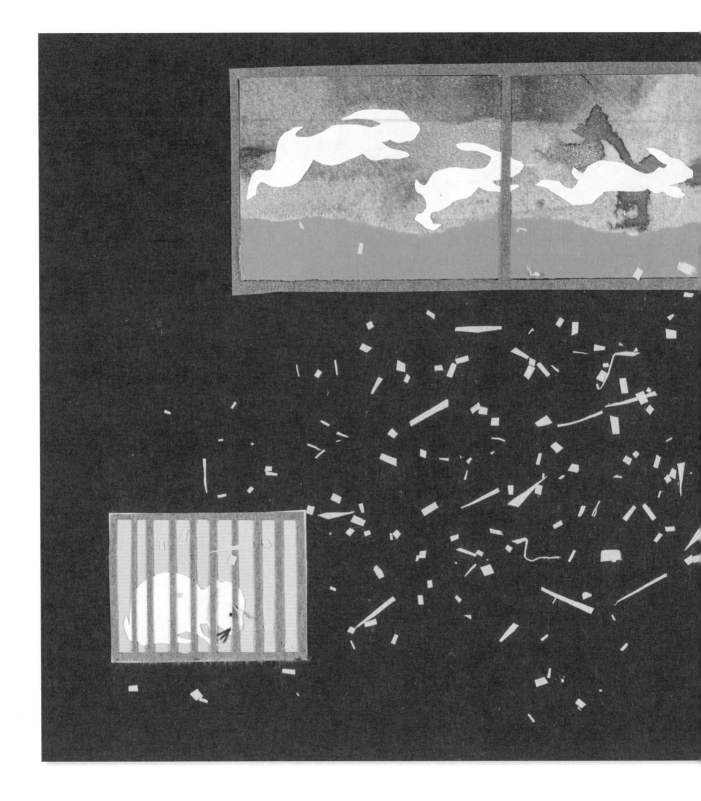

Over the land in a lab was a flop-eared bunny,
Part of an experiment, used to make money.

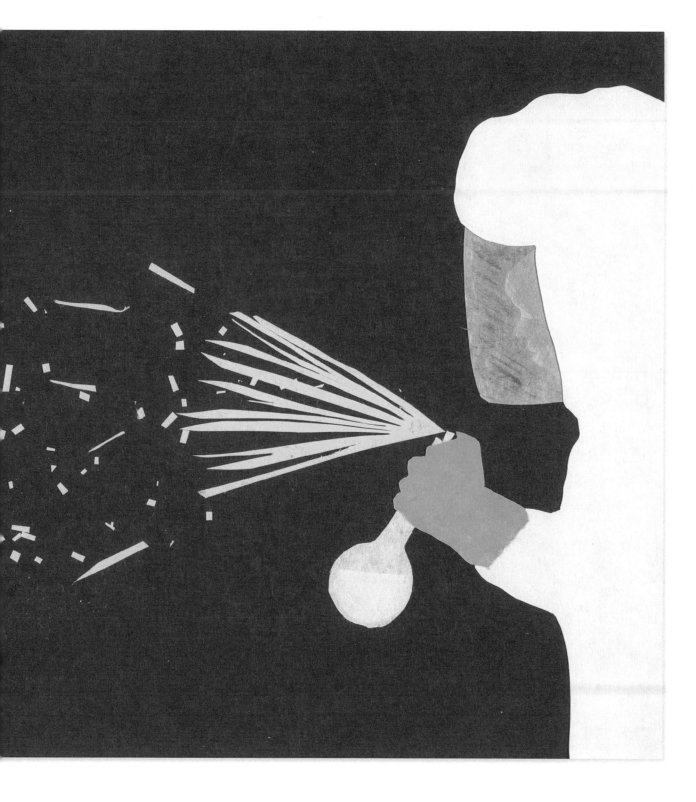

Eyes sprayed with make-up, she cried and cried,
'I wish ... I wish ... to be hopping outside.'

Bunny opened her eyes
And ... surprise, surprise:

She hopped out of a burrow
To greet the sunrise.

That night I dreamt of miraculous things:
Of bunnies on roller skates, horses with wings,
There were pigs on surfboards, riding on waves,

And dozens of chooks diving in caves.
The animals were happy, a smile on each face,
And Morella and I were setting the pace!